Come to the Apple

by Mary Lindeen • illustrated by Indie Penny

Do you have a paper?
You can come.

Do you have a lunch?
You can come.

Do you have a backpack?
You can come.

Do you have a hat?
You can come.

8

Do you have a friend?
You can come.

11

Do you have a seat?
You can come.

Do you have a color?

You can come.

You can come
to the apple farm!